Put Beginning Readers on the Right Track with
ALL ABOARD READING™

The All Aboard Reading series is especially for beginning readers. Written by noted authors and illustrated in full color, these are books that children really and truly *want* to read—books to excite their imagination, tickle their funny bone, expand their interests, and support their feelings. With four different reading levels, All Aboard Reading lets you choose which books are most appropriate for your children and their growing abilities.

Picture Readers—for Ages 3 to 6
Picture Readers have super-simple texts with many nouns appearing as rebus pictures. At the end of each book are 24 flash cards—on one side is the rebus picture; on the other side is the written-out word.

Level 1—for Preschool through First Grade Children
Level 1 books have very few lines per page, very large type, easy words, lots of repetition, and pictures with visual "cues" to help children figure out the words on the page.

Level 2—for First Grade to Third Grade Children
Level 2 books are printed in slightly smaller type than Level 1 books. The stories are more complex, but there is still lots of repetition in the text and many pictures. The sentences are quite simple and are broken up into short lines to make reading easier.

Level 3—for Second Grade through Third Grade Children
Level 3 books have considerably longer texts, use harder words and more complicated sentences.

All Aboard for happy reading!

D1045485

Library of Congress Cataloging-in-Publication Data

Del Prado, Dana.
    Terror below! : true shark stories / by Dana del Prado ; illustrated by Stephen Marchesi.
       p.   cm. — (All aboard reading)
    Summary: Presents facts and true stories about sharks and discusses both the good and the bad things they can do.
    1. Sharks—Juvenile literature.   2. Shark attacks—Juvenile literature.   [1. Sharks. 2. Shark attacks.]   I. Marchesi, Stephen, ill.   II. Title.   III. Series.
QL638.9.D43   1997
597'.31—dc20   96-35807
                                                   CIP
                                                    AC

ISBN 0-448-41124-5 A B C D E F G H I J

ALL
ABOARD
READING™
Level 3
Grades 2-3

TERROR BELOW!
True Shark Stories

By Dana del Prado
Illustrated by Stephen Marchesi

Grosset & Dunlap • New York

Are you afraid of sharks? Lots of people are. But you don't have to worry about them every time you go swimming. Shark attacks happen much less often in real life than they do in books or movies. In fact, there are fewer than 100 shark attacks a year in the whole world. Bee stings kill more people than sharks do.

Actually, sharks have more to fear from
humans than the other way around.
People kill hundreds of millions of sharks
every year. Some are eaten as food. Some
are caught by accident in giant fishing
nets. And some are hunted just for fun.

Many people think the world would be better off without sharks. But sharks do a lot of good. They help keep the ocean clean by eating up dead, sick, and weak animals—from tiny fish to huge whales. Some scientists believe that studying sharks will help them develop life-saving medicines.

Of course, sharks <u>are</u> dangerous. Hopefully, the three stories in this book are the closest you'll ever come to one!

Big and Little

The largest fish in the world is a shark—the whale shark. It grows to 35 or 40 feet, longer than a bus. Its mouth alone is six feet wide! But it is harmless. The whale shark has even let divers ride on its back.

The tiniest shark is only six inches long. It has a very long name, tsurana-gakobitosame. (It's fun to try to say it: Sur-AH-na-gak-oh-BIT-oh-SAH-mee.) This is Japanese for "little shark with a long face."

The Big Three

There are about 350 different kinds of sharks. New kinds are always being discovered. Luckily, only a few types attack people. These are the most dangerous:

great white shark

bull shark

tiger shark

Are there other dangerous sharks? Yes. But these are less likely to bother humans:

dusky

lemon

gray reef

hammerhead

mako

Hawaii, 1992

It was 7:30 in the morning. Rick had the beach all to himself. Not a soul was out. Soon he had to be at his job as a building worker. But he figured he had time to catch a few waves. That was the great thing about living in Hawaii. The surf was always nearby.

Huge breakers were crashing into shore. Rick grabbed his surfboard and dove in. Seconds later, he was riding a big wave. He caught another, and another.

There was just time for one more ride before work. Rick floated on his board waiting for the next really big one. As he drifted, he looked down into the clear blue water. A dark shape glided near him. It was a giant green sea turtle. Rick was a nature-lover. He knew he was very lucky to have seen such a rare sea creature.

Rick was still smiling when a larger
shadow drifted by. He couldn't quite make
it out. It wasn't a sea turtle. But what was
it? Then the water swirled. Up rose an
enormous tiger shark!

The shark opened its huge jaws. Rick could see row after row of jagged white teeth. Then those teeth came down hard. The shark bit into Rick's surfboard! The board swung up and down, back and forth as the shark shook it. Rick just held on tight with his arms and legs.

Suddenly Rick heard a loud SNAP. The tiger shark had bitten right through the board!

Rick knew he had to act . . . fast! He started paddling for shore. It felt like the longest swim of his life.

Finally he was there. A crowd was waiting. A busload of tourists had stopped to see what was going on in the water.

Rick was still scared. He hadn't been hurt at all. But one look at his chomped board was enough to start him shaking.

Why had the shark gone after the board and not Rick? Rick had no idea. But he was sure of one thing. He was very lucky.

Yum

What do sharks eat? Almost anything!
All these things have been found inside
sharks' stomachs:
    tin cans
    a crocodile head
    a wallet
    a drum
    cigarette packs
    nuts and bolts
    a suit of armor
    a fur coat

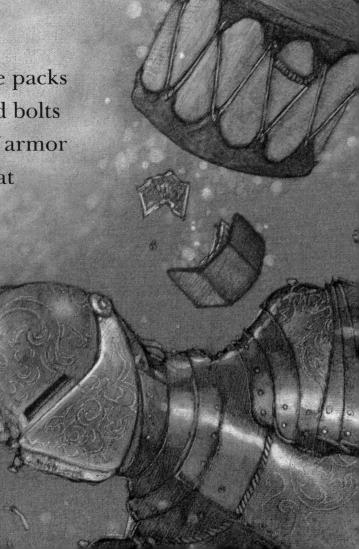

Australia, 1937

Iona had an unusual job. He was a pearl diver. Every day he swam the waters off the Great Barrier Reef in Australia, looking for oysters. He brought up hundreds in hopes of finding one that would hold a pearl.

One morning he dropped off the dive boat as usual. The water was warm and clear. It was easy to see oysters on rocks and in branches of white coral. There was a big one! Iona pried it off, then swam back up and left his catch in a bucket. He didn't open the oyster right then. He would do that later.

Down Iona went again. He swam slowly, searching hard for more oysters. Then, out of nowhere, a shadow appeared on the ocean floor. It loomed up behind him. Iona turned.

He was face-to-face with a giant tiger shark.

In a flash, the shark opened his huge
jaws and clamped them down around
Iona's neck. His head was inside the
shark's great dark mouth!

Iona was still alive. But he felt the shark's teeth closing down on him. He had just seconds to fight back. And he knew what to do. He felt around the shark's head. With all his strength, he stuck his thumbs deep into the shark's eyes! He pushed deeper and deeper. The shark thrashed in the water. Then it let go!

Iona was free. He sprang up to the surface. The other divers pulled him onto the dive boat. He was badly hurt. His neck was ringed with deep cuts.

There was no time to lose. The crew rushed Iona to the nearest hospital. It took 100 stitches to fix his wound.

The shark left scars around Iona's throat—like a necklace. But Iona was okay. He could go back to pearl diving. He even had something to remember that horrible day. It wasn't a pearl. It was a shark's tooth. Doctors had found it buried deep in Iona's neck.

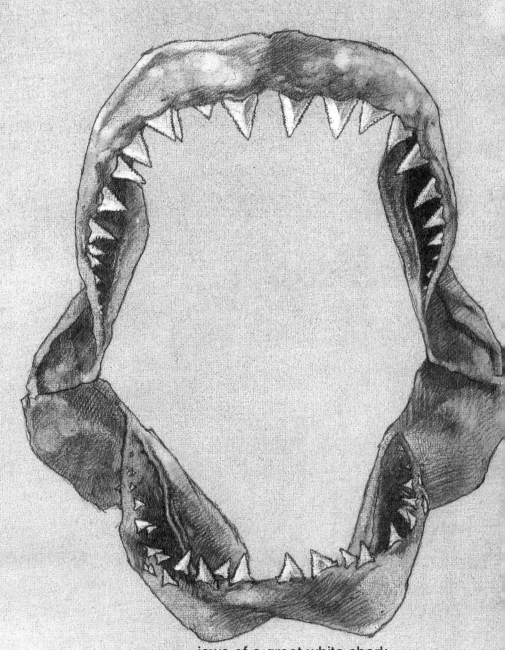

jaws of a great white shark

Teeth

A shark may lose thousands of teeth in its lifetime—some lose about a tooth a week. But sharks always have plenty of teeth. New ones keep taking the place of the teeth that fall out.

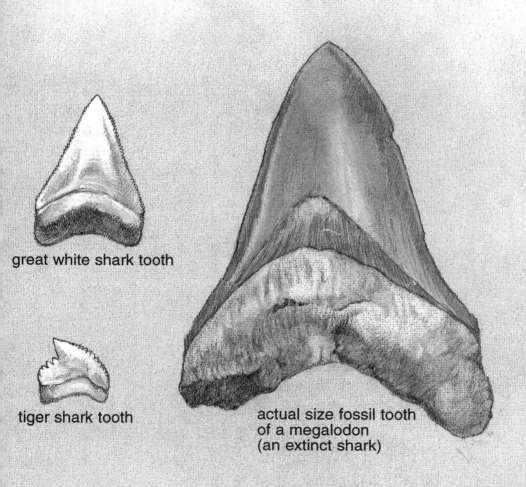

great white shark tooth

tiger shark tooth

actual size fossil tooth of a megalodon (an extinct shark)

Shark Chaser

Wouldn't it be great to have a pill that you could drop into the water—and make sharks go away from you? The U.S. Navy actually came up with one in the 1940s. It was called Shark Chaser. There was a problem, though. Shark Chaser did not work on all kinds of sharks. And it was useless against a feeding frenzy—when a group of hungry, excited sharks attack together.

South Australia, 1963

More than anything, Rodney wanted to win the spearfishing championship. He had won the year before. He knew he could do it again.

But so far he had had hardly any luck. He hadn't caught much at all. To take first place he'd have to bring down a truly huge fish.

Suddenly, Rodney saw a dusky morwong—it was big. This could win him the contest! The fish was just ahead of him. Rodney lifted his spear and took a shot.

He missed. The morwong swam off with a flip of its tail.

There were only minutes left in the contest. Rodney knew it was now or never. He caught sight of a school of barracuda. This was his last chance. He moved after them. Behind him the water was strangely still. At first he kept his eyes on the barracuda. But the quiet started to bother him. He looked over his shoulder.

There was a great white shark! Before Rodney could get away, the shark's huge mouth closed over his chest and back.

Terrified, Rodney used his free hand to beat at the shark's head. But the thick-skinned shark barely noticed. It shook Rodney back and forth in the water. Rodney tried to claw at the shark's black unblinking eye. But his hand slipped and his arm went straight into the shark's mouth. Still full of fight, Rodney tore his arm back out.

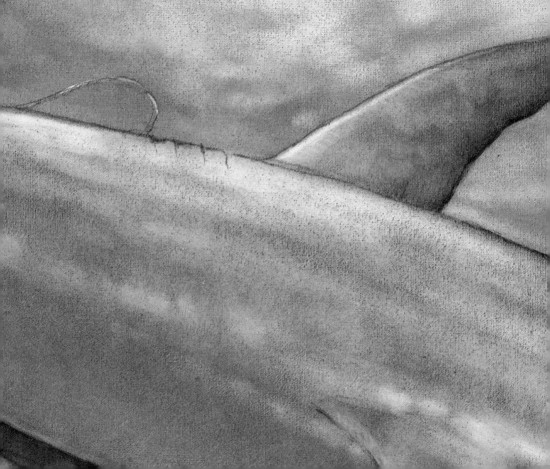

For the first time that day, Rodney had some luck. The great white let go. But it hadn't given up. The killer came after Rodney again. This time it gripped onto a float tied to Rodney's dive belt. The float was filled with dead fish Rodney used to attract his spearfishing targets.

Down, down the shark dragged him in the water. Rodney grabbed for the catch to undo his belt. Then the shark's razorlike teeth sawed through the line. Free once more, Rodney used the last of his strength to swim to the surface.

Luckily, a dive boat was just yards away. The crew pulled Rodney out of the water and onto the deck. He was bleeding badly.

The boat raced to shore. Soon Rodney was rushed to the nearest hospital. There a doctor worked on him for four hours. It took 462 stitches to save Rodney's life.

After a day like that, you would think Rodney would hate sharks. Not at all. Today he fights to protect them. And he runs a dive shop that takes people out to get a close look at sharks in the wild. Just not <u>too</u> close.

Doctor Shark

Sharks are healthy animals. Their wounds heal fast. They almost never get cancer. So scientists study sharks to learn new ways to help cure people.

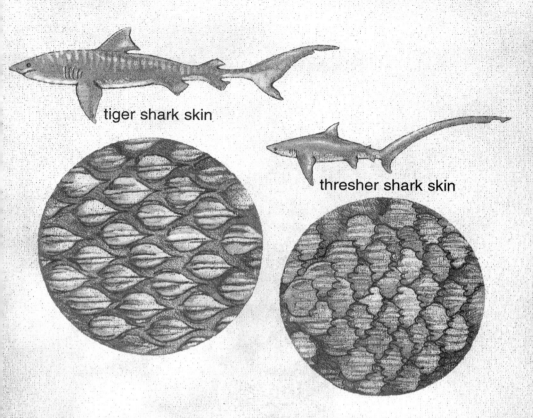

tiger shark skin

thresher shark skin

Shark Skin: Never Pet a Shark!

Did you know you can cut yourself
on a shark's skin? That has actually
happened to some swimmers. How?
A shark's skin is covered with sharp
toothlike prickles. If you pet a shark (a
bad idea!) from its head toward its tail, it
would feel smooth. Pet it from its tail
toward its head and—ouch!

Swimming with Sharks

If you play it safe, you can reduce the chance of a close encounter of the worst kind. Here are five rules to remember when swimming in places where sharks have been spotted:

1) Never swim alone.
2) Never swim with an open wound. Blood attracts sharks.
3) Never swim at night or at sunset.
4) Leave the water right away if a shark is spotted. Swim as smoothly as possible.
5) Never grab or injure any shark.